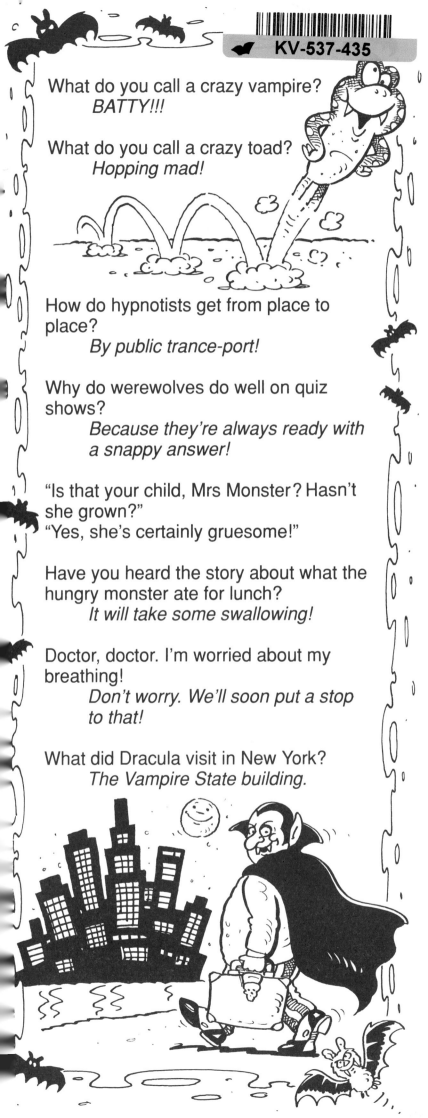

What do you call a crazy vampire?
BATTY!!!

What do you call a crazy toad?
Hopping mad!

How do hypnotists get from place to place?
By public trance-port!

Why do werewolves do well on quiz shows?
Because they're always ready with a snappy answer!

"Is that your child, Mrs Monster? Hasn't she grown?"
"Yes, she's certainly gruesome!"

Have you heard the story about what the hungry monster ate for lunch?
It will take some swallowing!

Doctor, doctor. I'm worried about my breathing!
Don't worry. We'll soon put a stop to that!

What did Dracula visit in New York?
The Vampire State building.

What activity association do young girl gargoyles go to?

The Frownies!

What do you do to join Dracula's fan club?

Write your name, address, age and blood group on the back of a stamped addressed envelope!

What do sea monsters eat?

Fish 'n' ships!

Where does Dracula keep his money?

In a blood bank!

Doctor: Do stop sucking your thumb, Frankie. Take it out of your mouth... I'll sew it back on in a minute!

How did the dinosaur pass his exams?

With extinction!

What do polite vampires say when you give them something?

Fang you!

1st Monster: What's the best thing for water on the brain?
2nd Monster: A tap on the head!

Frankie: I want a small mirror that I can carry around with me.
Shopkeeper: Do you want a hand mirror?
Frankie: No, I want to see my face as well!

THE SLIMY NOSE BY CONSTANT DRIPPING

The Giant Snake by ANNA CONDA

ACHES and PAINS by Arthur Ritis

THE BEAST WITH TALONS by Claud Body

NAUGHTY MONSTER by Enid Spanking

Building Dracula's CASTLE by Eva Brick

Vampire Fighting by IVOR CROSS

Beware of MONSTERS by LUKE AROUND

HELP ME by Linda Hand

SCARRED FOR LIFE by Mark Remains

HAPPY BIRTHDAY DRACULA BY ANNIE VERSARY

PREHISTORIC MONSTERS by Terry Dactyll

Snacks for Monsters by Ed Sam Widge

PUNCHED BY FRANKENSTEIN by Esau Stars

BATTLE WITH THE SPACE BEASTS by RAY GUNN

WOLFMAN'S HAIR CARE BOOK BY DAN DRUFF

Where do giant spiders play football?
At Webley Stadium!

1st Monster: My girlfriend is one of twins.
2nd Monster: Do you have trouble telling them apart?
1st Monster: Oh no! Her brother has a beard!

What do you give a seasick five-stomached monster?
As much room as possible!

"Don't eat with your fingers," said the Mummy monster to her child. "Use the shovel like everyone else!"

"Mum! Gran's out in the garden fighting with a giant slimy monster!"
"Never mind. I'm sure Gran won't hurt it too much!"

Did you hear about the stupid man who had a brain transplant?
The brain rejected him!

Who can you trust with a secret?
A mummy... they always keep things under wraps!

Dracula: How did you burn your ears, Frankie?
Frankie: I was listening to the match!

Did you hear about the unlucky princess?
> *She kissed a handsome prince and he turned into a toad!*

What is a monster football team called?
> *Slitherpool!*

Was Dracula married?
> *No, he was a **bat**chelor!*

Frankie: Do you have holes in your socks, Wolf Man?
Wolf Man: No, of course I don't.
Frankie: Then how do you get your feet in?

Where does the Abominable Snowman
go for a dance?
    To a snowball!

Which monster has the best hearing
of all?
    The eeriest!

What trees do monsters like best?
    Ceme-trees!

Why did the Invisible Man look in the
mirror?
    To make sure that he wasn't there!

Why did the monster schoolboy swallow
a coin?
    It was his dinner money!

WHAT DO YOU GET IF YOU CROSS A SPIDER WITH A DUCK?

What do you get if you cross a clock with a werewolf?
A watch-dog!

What do you get if you cross a mummy with a vampire!
A bandage that sucks blood!

What do you get if you cross a giant ape beast with egg-whites and sugar?
A meringue-utan!

What do you get if you cross a vampire with a parrot?
Something that bites you then says, "Who's a pretty boy then?"

What do you get if you cross a dwarf with a vampire?
Teeth marks in your kneecaps!

What do you get if you cross a crooked monster with a cement mixer?
A hardened criminal!

What do you get if you cross a crocodile with a fire-breathing monster?
A snapdragon!

Monster Boy: What lovely eyes you have!
Monster Girl: Thank you. Would you like one?

WEBBED FEET!

What do you call spiders who have just got married?
Newly-webs!

"Where's my shirt, Mum?" yelled Master Monster.
"Have you made my tea?" asked Miss Monster.
"Have you seen the newspaper?" said Mr Monster.
"THAT'S ENOUGH!" cried Mrs Monster.
"I've only got six pairs of hands!"

What does the Abominable Snowman say when he doesn't think something is possible?
Snow way!

What do you use to stop the Woolly Mammoth Monster charging?
A trunkquilliser!

Frankie: Can I have some birdseed?
Dracula: But you don't own a bird!
Frankie: I thought I'd try and grow one!

What do you call a deadly poisonous snake that's just bitten its own lip?
Doomed!

How do monsters count up to thirteen?
On their fingers!

What do you get if you mix pasta and the Abominable Snowman?
Spag-yeti!

What's the biggest moth of all?
A mammoth!

What sort of word puzzles do vampires hate?
Cross-words!

What do you call a blood-sucking bat that crashes into a fruit tree?
A jam-pire!

Boy: Why do all the children at school say I'm a werewolf?
Mother: You must ignore them – now go and comb your face!

What is an executioner's favourite meal?
He likes a good chop!

What did the man say when he was told he would be put on the torture rack?
Looks like I'm in for a long stretch!

Werewolf: I can't hear you. Please speak up!
Barber: I said I'm sorry but I've just cut one of your ears off!

What kind of ships do vampires like?
Blood vessels!

WHAT DO YOU CALL...?

What do you call a monster with a spade in his head?
Doug!

What do you call a monster with a large flat face made out of rock?
Cliff!

What do you call a monster with a tile on her head?
Ruth!

What do you call a monster floating on the surface of the water?
Bob!

What do you call a monster who always steals things?
Rob!

What do you call a monster swinging on a goalpost?
Annette!

What do you call a monster who looks like a duck?
Bill!

Why is Dracula such a nuisance?
He's a pain in the neck!

Wolfman: How do you join the police?
Frankie: Handcuff them together!

Why does a bald monster never have any keys?
He's lost all his locks!

How do you start a race of giant grizzly bears?
Say ready, teddy, go!

Can a toothless vampire bite you?
No, but he can give you a nasty suck!

What do space monsters have for breakfast?
Unidentified frying objects!

What game do little vampires like to play?
Bat's cradle!

Wolfman: What would we have if all the cars in this land were painted red?
Dracula: A red car-nation!

What do elves do after school?
Gnomework!

Which burns longer – the candles on Wolfman's birthday cake or the candles on the Mummy's cake?
Neither – all candles burn shorter!

Monster: How much is a haircut?
Barber: £4.
Monster: How much is a shave?
Barber: £2.
Monster: Shave my head, will you?

What do invisible people drink?
> *Evaporated milk!*

Why can you never play practical jokes on snakes?
> *You can't pull their legs!*

Why do dragons sleep during the day?
> *They like to hunt knights!*

What do you call a war between groups of vampires?
> *A bat-tle!*

Frankie: I'm off to bed now.
Dracula: Why are you taking a pencil with you?
Frankie: I want to draw the curtains!

How do you break down the door to Dracula's castle?
Use a bat-tering ram!

Did you hear that the Leopard Man tried to creep out of his cage without anyone seeing him?
He was spotted!

On which side does Wolfman have most hair?
The outside!

What do you get when a demon starts to explain how to do something?
A demon-stration!

Did you hear about the monster who had a watch strapped to every finger?
He had time on his hands!

Dracula: How did you manage to stab your foot?
Frankie: There was a fork in the road!

RIDDLES FROM THE CRAZY CRYPT

What happened when the axe fell on Frankie's head?
There was an axe-i-dent!

What occurs once in a month, twice in a moment but never in a day?
The letter M!

What party game does Dr Jekyll like to play?
Hyde and Seek!

What do cannibals eat for breakfast when they come to stay?
Buttered host!

When is it bad luck to be followed by a black cat?
When you're a mouse!

What goes up and down but never moves?
Stairs!

What can you break without even touching it?
A promise!

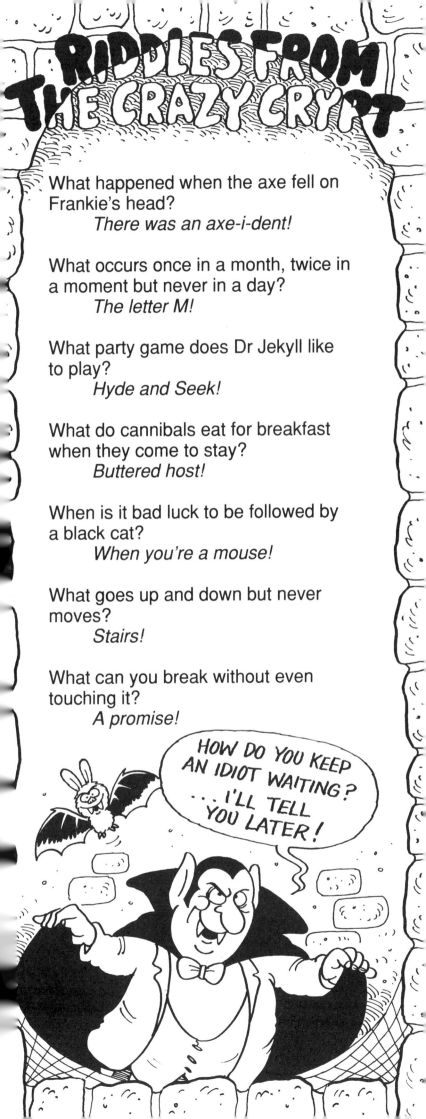

What do you give Dracula's grandad on his two hundredth birthday?
A cake with two hundred candles and a fire extinguisher!

Monster 1: What is always walking on its head?
Monster 2: A nail in your shoe!

What do you get if you cross a wizard with a length of rope?
Spellbound!

How do vampires like their fish served?
In bat-ter!

Frankie: Have you any chips left?
Chip Shop Man: Yes, lots!
Frankie: Serves you right for frying too many!

What are the largest ants in the world?
Gi-ants!

Monster: What do you charge for dinner?
Waiter: £10 a head!
Monster: Then bring me a couple of ears!

Why aren't vampires very good at telling lies?

They can't cross their fingers!

Monster Teacher: Can you say your alphabet for me?
Monster Child: A, M, H, N, O ....
Monster Teacher: Where did you learn to say your alphabet like that?
Monster Child: At the opticians!

Did you hear about the race between the giant jellyfish?

It had to be abandoned when the starter said, "Get set"!

Do you have any brontosaurus sandwiches?

Sorry, we're out of bread!

What does a vampire do if he only has one fang?

Grin and bare it!

Frankie: I keep dreaming about large red monsters with green teeth!
Dracula: Have you seen a doctor?
Frankie: No, just large red monsters with green teeth!